This book belongs to

The Jelly That Wouldn't Wobble
An original concept by author Angela Mitchell
© Angela Mitchell
Illustrated by Sarah Horne

MAVERICK ARTS PUBLISHING LTD
Studio 11, City Business Centre, 6 Brighton Road, Horsham,
West Sussex, RH13 5BB, +44 (0)1403 256941
© Maverick Arts Publishing Limited
First published 2012
New edition published October 2019

ISBN 978-1-84886-459-7

Maverick
publishing
www.maverickbooks.co.uk

The JELLY That Wouldn't WOBBLE

Written by
Angela Mitchell

Illustrated by
Sarah Horne

Princess Lolly wriggled with excitement.

It was her 89th birthday party.

"Where's my special *jelly*?" she asked.

"Here, Your Highness!" replied the guard, as the cook and his assistant carried in her special jelly.

Everyone gasped with delight.
It was glorious!

Princess Lolly squealed with excitement, prodded the jelly and then looked puzzled. She prodded the jelly again...

"This jelly **doesn't wobble!**" exclaimed Princess Lolly in horror. The cook prodded the jelly too.

"Doesn't wobble? Doesn't wobble?" flustered the cook. "Of course it wobbles, Your Highness: it's *jelly!*"

"I. SAY. THIS. JELLY. DOESN'T. WOBBLE!"

sobbed the princess.

She prodded the jelly again and again...
It still didn't wobble!

"I want my jelly to wobble!

Make it wobble!
WHY. WON'T. MY.
JELLY. WOBBLE?!"

Everyone looked at the jelly in wonder.

"I don't want to be eaten!" growled the jelly.

"Not be eaten?" boomed the princess.
"MELT IT!"

"Your Highness, NO!" begged the cook.

"Think of the mess, Your Highness," said the guard.

Princess Lolly pondered for a moment.

I RULE!

"A thousand and one chocolate sovereigns for anyone who can make this jelly wobble!" announced the princess.

"I'll prod it with my walking stick!" said the oldest guest.

That didn't work.

"Rock the table!" shouted the twin guests.

That didn't work.

"Scare it!" the royal window cleaner hollered and pulled some horrible faces.

That didn't work.

The jelly **still** wouldn't wobble.

Princess Lolly turned the colour of a very ripe strawberry.
The cook turned white with worry.

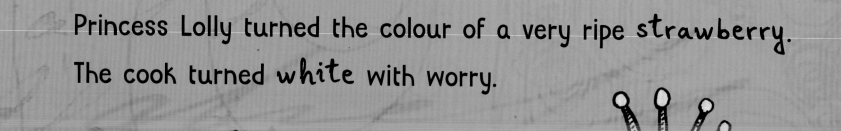

"I know how to make it wobble," said the smallest guest.

"You do?"
boomed the princess.

"You do?"
questioned the cook.

"You do?"
repeated the cook's assistant.

"Yes, Your Highness," said the smallest guest proudly.
"Make the jelly really, really, reaaally cold.
It will shiver and **have** to wobble!"

"Wonderful!" said the cook.

"Proceed!" commanded Princess Lolly.

The cook froze for a moment.

"Ice cream, ice cream,"
whispered the smallest guest.
"Of course!" gasped the cook.

There was a great scurry while a rather **wobbly**, old ladder and the royal ice cream scoop were fetched.

Tottering on the top of the ladder, the cook placed three scoops of **tutti frutti** ice cream on top of the jelly's crown.

Everyone held their breath, and watched as the jelly
tried very hard not to shiver...

Suddenly, the jelly jerked.

"I saw something move!" gasped the smallest guest.

"Oh, please wobble," begged the cook.

"Brrrrrr!" The jelly suddenly shivered.
"Brrrrrrrrrrrrrrrrrrr!
Brrrrrrrrrrrrrrrrrrr!"

It shivered again, rocking this way and that, quivering and quaking, trembling and shaking.

What a spectacle!

The guests moved back in fear,
the cook began to cry,
and Princess Lolly stared in wonder at this
quivering, shivering sight as the defeated jelly...

...wobbled and wibbled, wibbled and wobbled, just as a royal jelly should!

The hungry guests cheered, the cook sobbed with relief, and the guard stood at ease.

"Silence!" cried Princess Lolly. There was an instant hush.

"Now we can eat jelly!" she proclaimed.
"Phew," sighed the cook, consoled.

And they did.

(And, by the way, the Princess kept her promise
and rewarded the smallest guest with
a thousand and one chocolate sovereigns).